JACKSONVILLE

JAGUARS

BY JOSH ANDERSON

Stride
An Imprint of The Child's World®
childsworld.com

The Child's World
childsworld.com

Published by The Child's World®
800-599-READ • www.childsworld.com

Photography Credits
Cover: © Carmen Mandato / Staff / Getty Images; page 1: © Africa Studio / Shutterstock; page 3: © Trask Smith/Cal Sport Media / Newscom; page 5: © Rob Carr / Staff / Getty Images; page 6: © Andy Lyons / Staff / Getty Images; page 9: © James Gilbert / Stringer / Getty Images; page 10: © Doug Benc / Staff / Getty Images; page 11: © stevezmina1 / Getty Images; page 12: © Chris Graythen / Staff / Getty Images; page 12: © Andy Lyons / Staff / Getty Images; page 13: © Sam Greenwood / Staff / Getty Images; page 13: © Andy Lyons / Staff / Getty Images; page 14: © Al Messerschmidt / Staff / Getty Images; page 15: © Sam Greenwood / Staff / Getty Images; page 16: © Scott Halleran / Staff / Getty Images; page 16: © Doug Benc / Staff / Getty Images; page 17: © Jeff Gross / Staff / Getty Images; page 17: © Al Bello / Staff / Getty Images; page 18: © Doug Pensinger / Staff / Getty Images; page 18: © Elias Shoemake / UPI Photo Service / Newscom; page 19: © Kevin C. Cox / Staff / Getty Images; page 19: © Handout / Getty Images; page 20: © Wesley Hitt / Stringer / Getty Images; page 20: © Andy Lyons / Staff / Getty Images; page 21: © Sam Greenwood / Staff / Getty Images; page 21: © Greg Fiume / Stringer/ Getty Images; page 22: © Scott Halleran / Staff / Getty Images; page 23: © Sam Greenwood / Staff / Getty Images; page 23: © stevezmina1 / Getty Images; page 25: © Jamie Squire / Staff / Getty Images; page 26: © Scott Halleran / Staff / Getty Images; page 29: © Joe Murphy / Stringer / Getty Images

ISBN Information
9781503857797 (Reinforced Library Binding)
9781503860520 (Portable Document Format)
9781503861886 (Online Multi-user eBook)
9781503863248 (Electronic Publication)

LCCN 2021952669

Printed in the United States of America

BRINGING THE WORLD TO YOUNG READERS 1968

TABLE OF CONTENTS

GO JAGUARS!

The Jacksonville Jaguars compete in the National Football **League's** (NFL's) American Football Conference (AFC). They play in the AFC South **division**, along with the Houston Texans, Indianapolis Colts, and Tennessee Titans. The "Jags" are the only major professional sports team to play in Jacksonville. In 2021, the team had the chance to select first in the NFL Draft and chose Trevor Lawrence, an exciting young quarterback who made headlines at Clemson University. Let's learn more about the Jaguars!

AFC SOUTH DIVISION

Houston Texans

Indianapolis Colts

Jacksonville Jaguars

Tennessee Titans

THE JAGUARS HAVE MADE THE PLAYOFFS SEVEN TIMES IN TEAM HISTORY.

BECOMING THE JAGUARS

The Jaguars began play as an **expansion team** in 1995. Many fans submitted ideas for the team's name. The oldest living jaguar in North America lived in the Jacksonville Zoo. That's part of the reason Jaguars was chosen as the team name. While they've never played in the **Super Bowl**, they were very successful in their early years. The team made the **playoffs** in four of its first five seasons. They even made it to the AFC Championship Game twice during that time.

QUARTERBACK MARK BRUNELL PLAYED IN THE JAGUARS' VERY FIRST GAME IN 1995.

BY THE NUMBERS

THREE
trips to the AFC Championship Game for the Jaguars

The Jaguars have won
THREE
division titles.

417
points scored by the team in 2017—a Jaguars record!

14
wins for the Jaguars in 1999

AFTER WINNING THE AFC SOUTH DIVISION IN 2017, THE JAGS CAME WITHIN ONE WIN OF REACHING THE SUPER BOWL.

TIAA BANK FIELD IS NEXT TO THE ST. JOHNS RIVER IN DOWNTOWN JACKSONVILLE, FLORIDA.

GAME DAY

The Jaguars play their home games at TIAA Bank Field. The **stadium** has been their home since the team started play in 1995. About 67,000 fans can fit inside to cheer on the Jaguars. In 2005, TIAA Bank Field hosted Super Bowl 39 between the Philadelphia Eagles and the New England Patriots. It's also home to college football's Gator Bowl every year. Fans enjoy posing with the huge bronze Jaguar statue in front of the stadium entrance.

We're Famous!

One of the most passionate Jaguars fans ever just might be a fictional character! Actor Manny Jacinto played Jason Mendoza on NBC's comedy *The Good Place*. Mendoza frequently wore Jags gear and talked about his favorite player, quarterback Blake Bortles. Jacinto even made a trip in real life to a Jaguars playoff game in 2018.

UNIFORM

TEAL

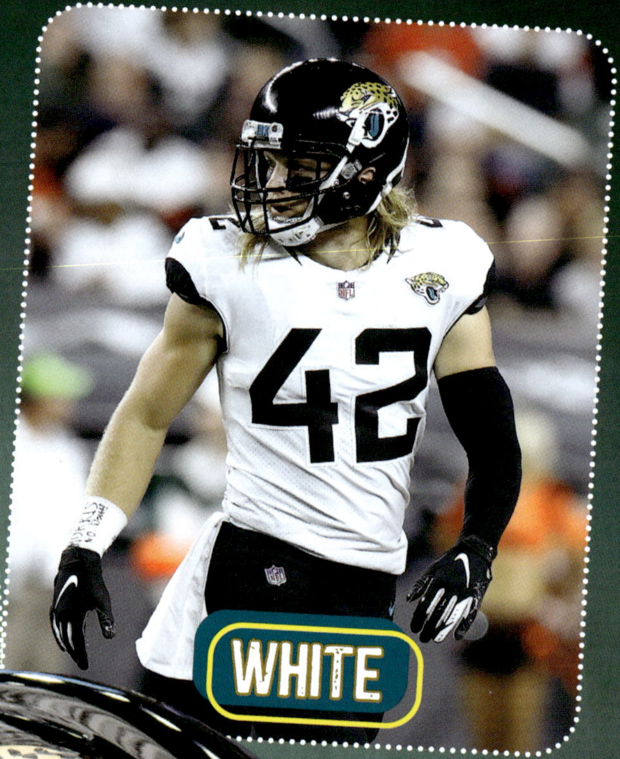
WHITE

Truly Weird

In a 2016 game against the Houston Texans, quarterback Blake Bortles caused an unlucky turnover. When he noticed that running back T. J. Yeldon was covered by a defender, Bortles wanted to avoid an interception. He tried to throw the ball into the ground at Yeldon's feet. Instead, the ball bounced off of Yeldon's foot and into the hands of a Houston defender!

Alternate Jersey

Sometimes teams wear an alternate jersey that is different from their home and away jerseys. It might be a bright color or have a unique theme. Jacksonville wore these all-gold uniforms for a 2016 game against the Tennessee Titans. The new look proved unlucky—the Jags lost the game.

JAGUARS PLAYERS RUN ONTO THE FIELD THROUGH TWO GIANT JAGUAR HEADS THAT CREATE A CLOUD OF SMOKE WHEN THEY ROAR.

TEAM SPIRIT

Going to a game at TIAA Bank Field can be a blast! You might think fans are booing, but they're actually shouting one of the team's most common chants: "Duuuuval." Duval is the name of the county where Jacksonville is located. Some Jags fans can enjoy one of the most unique NFL experiences. They can cheer for the Jags from one of the two swimming pools located above the north end zone. The Jacksonville ROAR cheerleading squad entertains the crowd at every game. They're joined by the team's mascot, Jaxson de Ville, a costumed yellow and teal jaguar.

JAXSON DE VILLE

HEROES OF HISTORY

Mark Brunell

Quarterback | 1995–2003

Brunell is the Jags franchise leader with 25,698 passing yards and 144 passing **touchdowns**. He led the team to 63 regular season victories and four playoff appearances. Brunell is the franchise's all-time leader in rushing yards for a quarterback with 2,219. He was selected for three **Pro Bowls** as a Jaguar.

Maurice Jones-Drew

Running Back | 2006–2013

Jones-Drew's 81 combined touchdowns are the most in franchise history. His 8,071 rushing yards rank second all-time in Jacksonville. In 2011, Jones-Drew led the league with 1,606 rushing yards. He had 15 rushing touchdowns in a season twice. Jones-Drew was selected for the Pro Bowl three times.

Jimmy Smith

Wide Receiver | 1995–2005

Smith's 12,287 receiving yards are most in Jaguars history and rank 26th all-time. He had nine seasons with at least 1,000 yards. His 116 catches in 1999 led the NFL. Smith's best career game was in 2000, when he logged 15 receptions, 291 receiving yards, and three touchdowns. He was picked for the Pro Bowl five times.

Fred Taylor

Running Back | 1998–2008

Taylor rushed for over 1,000 yards in seven different seasons. His 11,271 rushing yards are the most in Jaguars history. Overall, he ranks 17th all-time in rushing yards. Taylor helped lead the Jags to the playoffs four times. He was chosen for one Pro Bowl.

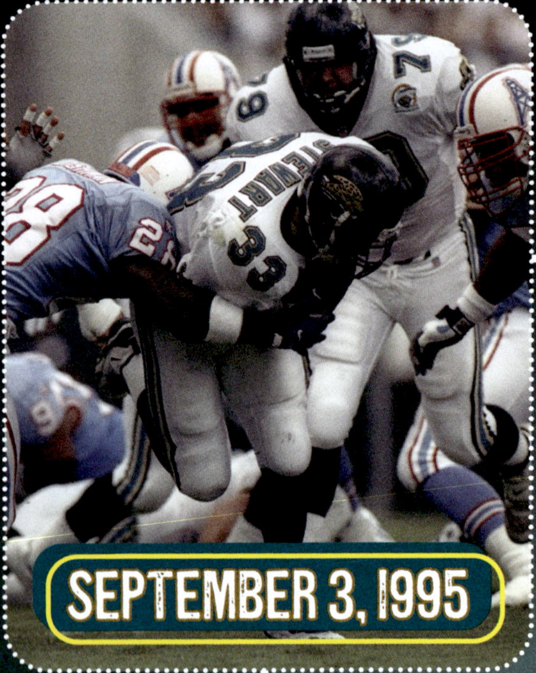

SEPTEMBER 3, 1995

Fans in Jacksonville witness the first game in Jaguars history. The Houston Oilers win 10–3.

JANUARY 15, 2000

The Jaguars defeat the Miami Dolphins 62–7 in a Divisional Round playoff game. It's the biggest playoff blowout in modern NFL history.

BIG DAYS

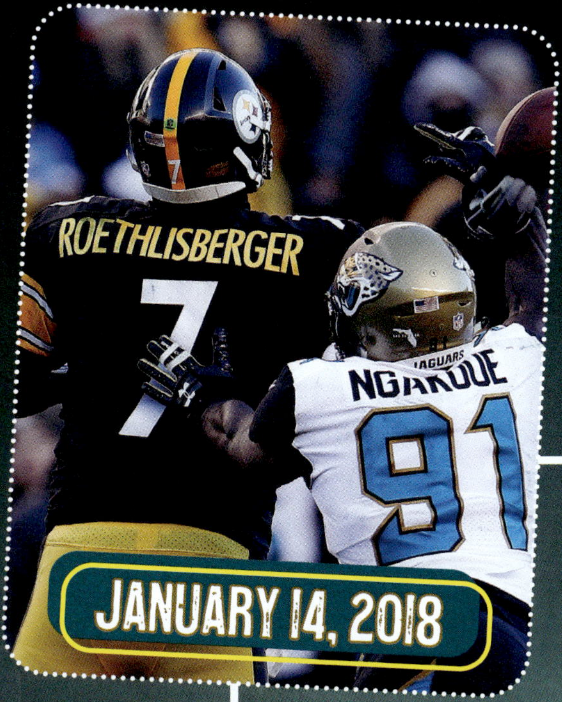

JANUARY 14, 2018

The Jags' 45–42 victory over the Pittsburgh Steelers gets them to the AFC Championship Game for the first time in 18 seasons.

APRIL 29, 2021

With the first pick in the NFL Draft, the Jaguars select Clemson University quarterback Trevor Lawrence.

MODERN-DAY MARVELS

Josh Allen

Defensive End | Debut: 2019

In 2019, Allen became the first Jaguars **rookie** ever chosen for the Pro Bowl. His 10.5 **sacks** were the most by any rookie in that season. Allen was named a team captain in 2020 before a knee injury ended his season early.

Trevor Lawrence

Quarterback | Debut: 2021

During his college career, Lawrence led the Clemson Tigers to the 2018 National Championship. The Jaguars selected Lawrence with the first overall pick of the 2021 NFL Draft. He threw for 332 yards and three touchdowns in his NFL debut.

James Robinson

Running Back | Debut: 2020

Robinson was picked as an All-Conference player three times during college. As a rookie in 2020, he rushed for 1,070 yards and seven touchdowns. His 1,414 total yards in 2020 were the most ever by an undrafted rookie.

Brandon Scherff

Offensive Guard | Debut: 2022

Scherff played his first seven seasons for the Washington Commanders. He signed with the Jaguars before the 2022 season. He's started every game he's played during his career. Scherff has been selected for the Pro Bowl five times. He's shown here in his old Commanders uniform.

TONY BOSELLI STARTED 90 OF THE 91 GAMES HE PLAYED FOR THE JAGUARS DURING HIS CAREER.

THE GOAT

GREATEST OF ALL TIME

TONY BOSELLI

Boselli is nicknamed the "Original Jaguar." He was a two-time All-American selection while playing at the University of Southern California. He became the Jaguars' first-ever college draft choice when they selected him second overall in the 1995 NFL Draft. Boselli started 90 games for the Jags in his career. He was chosen for the Pro Bowl five times. He also was chosen for the NFL's All-Decade Team for the 1990s.

FAN FAVORITE

Josh Scobee–Kicker

2004–2014

Scobee earned the love of the Jacksonville fan base with some huge kicks during his 11 seasons. He was called the "Colt Killer" for making several big kicks against the Jags' rival, the Indianapolis Colts. In 2011, he tied the NFL record with three field goals of more than 50 yards in the same game.

THE BIG GAME

JANUARY 4, 1997 – AFC DIVISIONAL PLAYOFF GAME

The Jaguars entered their playoff game against the Denver Broncos as heavy underdogs. It was only the team's second year playing in the NFL. Legendary quarterback John Elway led a talented Broncos team. Denver scored two touchdowns in the first quarter and led 12–0. Then the Jaguars came racing back. They scored the next 23 points in the game. Natrone Means rushed for 140 yards. Quarterback Mark Brunell sealed the Jaguars' victory with a 16-yard touchdown pass to Jimmy Smith in the fourth quarter. The Jags earned a trip to the AFC Championship Game with a 30–27 victory.

THE JAGUARS WERE THE LAST TEAM TO EVER DEFEAT LEGENDARY QUARTERBACK JOHN ELWAY IN A PLAYOFF GAME.

TOM COUGHLIN LED THE JAGUARS TO THE PLAYOFFS FOUR TIMES.

AMAZING FEATS

35 Touchdown Passes

In 2015 by QUARTERBACK Blake Bortles

13 Rushing Touchdowns

In 1999 by RUNNING BACK James Stewart

14 Receiving Touchdowns

In 2015 for WIDE RECEIVER Allen Robinson

14.5 Sacks

In 2017 for DEFENSIVE END Calais Campbell

ALL-TIME BEST

PASSING YARDS

Mark Brunell
25,698

Blake Bortles
17,646

David Garrard
16,003

RUSHING YARDS

Fred Taylor
11,271

Maurice Jones-Drew
8,071

James Stewart
2,951

RECEIVING YARDS

Jimmy Smith
12,287

Keenan McCardell
6,393

Marcedes Lewis
4,502

SACKS*

Tony Brackens
55

Yannick Ngakoue
37.5

Joel Smeenge
34

SCORING

Josh Scobee
1,022

Mike Hollis
764

Maurice Jones-Drew
486

INTERCEPTIONS

Rashean Mathis
30

Aaron Beasley
15

Donovin Darius
14

*unofficial before 1982

CORNERBACK RASHEAN MATHIS WAS CHOSEN FOR THE PRO BOWL AFTER THE 2006 SEASON.

GLOSSARY

division (dih-VIZSH-un): a group of teams within the NFL that play each other more frequently and compete for the best record

expansion team (ek-SPAN-shun TEEM): a new team added to the league

league (LEEG): an organization of sports teams that compete against each other

playoffs (PLAY-ahfs): a series of games played after the regular season that decides which two teams play in the Super Bowl

Pro Bowl (PRO BOWL): the NFL's All-Star game, where the best players in the league compete

rookie (RUH-kee): a player playing in his first season

sack (SAK): when a quarterback is tackled behind the line of scrimmage before he can throw the ball

stadium (STAY-dee-um): a building where teams play that has a field and seats for fans

Super Bowl (SOO-puhr BOWL): the championship game of the NFL, played between the winners of the AFC and NFC

touchdown (TUTCH-down): a play in which the ball is brought into the other team's end zone, resulting in six points

FIND OUT MORE

IN THE LIBRARY

Bulgar, Beth and Mark Bechtel. *My First Book of Football.* New York, NY: Time Inc. Books, 2015.

Jacobs, Greg. *The Everything Kids' Football Book, 7th Edition*. Avon, MA: Adams Media, 2021.

Sports Illustrated Kids. *The Greatest Football Teams of All Time*. New York, NY: Time Inc. Books, 2018.

Wyner, Zach. *Jacksonville Jaguars*. New York, NY: AV2 Books, 2020.

ON THE WEB

Visit our website for links about the Jacksonville Jaguars:
childsworld.com/links

Note to parents, teachers, and librarians: We routinely verify our web links to make sure they are safe and active sites. Encourage your readers to check them out!

INDEX

ABOUT THE AUTHOR

Josh Anderson has published over 50 books for children and young adults. His two boys are the greatest joys in his life. Hobbies include coaching his sons in youth basketball, no-holds-barred games of Apples to Apples, and taking long family walks. His favorite NFL team is a secret he'll never share!